Where Writers Grow Into Authors

HAND

ME

DOWNS

By Felisha Bradshaw

Written By: Felisha Bradshaw

Typeset/Layout by: Strawberry Publications, LLC |
www.StrawberrryPublications.com & UGMAG3

Cover Design by: Junnita Jackson

Urban Grapevine Publishing

DEDICATION

This book is dedicated to my wife Jerri Duncan Hansen.
You always say, "Go for it babe. You will make it happen."
So I picked back up the pen and finished what I started.

Thank you for the vote of confidence and the unwavering support!
You are my Lucky6 (insider)! I love you!
Love you for a Couple of Forever's.

HAND ME DOWNS

FELISHA BRADSHAW

Epilogue

BE CAREFUL WHAT YOU PRAY FOR

HAND ME DOWNS- (n.) particularly anything that has been handed down from one person to another, preferably known as "used goods".

Perhaps it's possible to meet someone who will turn your life around for the better just by two sets of eyes meeting, a coinciding double take, where each person's feeling the other is "the one". Women pray for this man of their dreams, a fairy tale and knight in shining armor. Some even take these prayers that are thrown up to God without specifications about what type of man they're looking for, and then settle for the first man who comes their way; assuming it was God that sent him. They forget that the devil is active and working overtime as well and he's one mean muthah fuckah destined to have his due.

Ritza prayed for a knight in shining armor for so long she was blinded by the glare she assumed came from his armor never noticing it was the glare from his mephitic and illusive sword. The man that came to set her free was cut from a cloth that would not free her from her old life, but instead, bind her captive in a new.

Blaze's swag smoked screened his interior personality. His "lady's man" aura was nothing compared to what lied beneath. Women were pawns in the games he played. The "Pussy for Sale" game was lucrative and he was all about paper baggin'. He had his hands in anything that would lead to a profit; loan sharking, numbers running, and drug trafficking. But what he loved the most was pimpin'. It wasn't so much the money he made from his bitches but, the logic of power he had over them mentally. He could turn the most sophisticated and refined woman into a bitch with a price tag on her pussy simply with a flash of his unblemished smile, deep dimples and promises of love and adventure. Hmmm, and the weak, well, they were like putty in his hands. So women beware, Blaze will send the life you know up in flames and have you forever burning in his pit, he calls the good life from just a mind fuck, a subliminal orgasm.

Be careful what you pray for and skittish of those who claim to be the answers to your prayers.

COLDEST WINTER EVER

"Ritza, I'm cold. Can't we go sleep in the basement like we use to."

Fallon trembled as the wind smacked against her face. Tears froze on her cheeks like morning dew in December from the zero below weather. This day seemed like the coldest winter ever, but that was farthest from the truth. Days like this would come again, and again in every season.

"Now Fallon listen, I told you before, so stop whining. You know what mama said."

Ritza tried to hold back harsh word towards her baby sister, because she too was cold and out of solutions. Her fingertips numb from the cold she pulled Fallon close, shielding her from the winter chill while cursing her mother under her breath and praying for someone to rescue her at the same time.

Roz Trell, was once a factory worker for Carpenter's Steel. After the company moved out of state it left her flat broke with two daughters and two sons. After running into Red, Roz thought her prayers were answered. Red held a full time job at Sikorsky Aircraft for over twenty years. He kept the bills and rent paid, her babies mouths fed and their backs warm. As the winter months settled in, she saw less of Red and more of the bills. Always missing in action three to four days out the week, Red finally came storming in reeking of liquor and a sweet unfamiliar smoky smell. Red seemed to care less about her well-being or whether her kids ate and more about his cravings.

"Red baby, can I get a few dollars to get the kids something to eat?"

Red didn't bother to answer Roz. He pulled out the last of his fifth of Gin, taking it to the head. The kids stared at Roz hungrily. Their eyes told tales of the growling monster lying in the depths of their tiny stomachs. Roz stood four feet eleven inches. Her curvaceous body and thick hips kept Red coming back each time. Her round plump ass; her greatest *asset* influenced Red's decision in her favor. Not your beauty queen, but she learned young, pussy didn't have a face and if worked properly it opened the door to all your needs and wants. She hated tricking with her man, but she realized ho'ing was part of the game: give a little something, get a little something. Ritza paid close attention to the way her mother frolicked her ass in front of Red before asking him again. Biting her bottom lip then slowly releasing it, Roz's palmed her hips and slid down centering her middle precisely on the mound growing in Red's lap. Her eyes glistened as she fought her shame-filled emotions from surfacing.

"'Come on Daddy Red. What I gotta do to get some change from you?' She detected Red's small dick rise in his saturated oily pants. She leaned in and whispered, poking out her chest, "Tell me what Daddy wants his bitch to do. I gotchoo, baby. You want this ass wrapped around your big dick? Imagining me sitting on your fat dick has this pussy wet and slippery. You ready to fall in?"

Red couldn't resist. He loved the way she stroked his ego. Better yet, he loved the way she stroked his dick between her thick ass cheeks. He reached in his pocket and pulled out a wad of singles.

"Ritza and Troy, go and get some Chinese food for ya'll. Dante you take Fallon and get her outtah them day clothes and into some PJ's.'

The kids scattered upon his demands, mainly excited because they were going to eat. Ritza took the money from Red's hand. She wanted to thank her mother with her eyes, but Roz refused to look up at her.

"Troy, be careful and hold your sister's hand."

Troy sucked his teeth and mumbled as he walked. He hated holding Ritza's hand in public. Everyone assumed she was his girlfriend. Friends and strangers alike would walk up to him and say foul shit like, 'Damn Baby T, you got a fine ass Shorty. I know you be banging that fat ass out.' He'd never said anything back. He released Ritza's hand just as they reached the block, as if it was filthy. She never understood why. She thought he was ashamed of her thrift store hand me down clothes and the fact she always looked like a charity case. Troy never fell shy of flashy. His father always made sure of that. But his belly grumbled like the rest of his siblings. As for Ritza and Fallon's father, he disappeared long ago. For the most part when he did surface he claimed broke.

The only thing her father ever gave to her was her coal colored eyes. She had a matured body like a sixteen year old. She skipped training bras, straight to wearing a "B" cup. Her hips were an inherited trait. She got them from her momma. It was the one thing that finalized everyone's assumptions.

"Troy, why Ma always gotta give up something to get something out of Red. Aint she like trickin'?" Ritza looked up at her brother for the answer.

"Girl, that ain't none of your business and let me make one thing clear you can't trick for what is rightfully yours.'" Those words stuck with Ritza all the way into adulthood.

GAME OVER

Lately, Red just couldn't seem to manage his money. His gambling habit and his other addictive habits seemed to eat up his healthy paycheck each week before he got the chance to give Roz money for rent. And, he recognized long ago she'd hold out on giving up her sweet pussy if he didn't come through with some cash. All he needed was a way out.

"Hey what's up Blaze? Let me shoot something your way, nephew." Blaze pushed his bottom bitch off his lap and offered his no good beggin' uncle a seat.

"What is it now? You always want something for nothing, and I ain't in that business?"

Red exhausted free funds from his nephew and had to come at him from a business angle. "Nah Nephew, I have a proposition for you. All I need is a few dollars on consignment. I'mma give you some future for something in the here and now."

Blaze frowned at his uncle running game. *Don't this old head know you can't play a playah.* He snapped his finger beckoning his bottom bitch. "We're out! Let's go!" Red stumbled behind him.

"Look nephew, I am sure you're always looking for new bitches and I have the ultimate bitch for you. She's a bit young, but in a year or two she can be picked up. I'm talking 'bout a fine piece of ass, needy and looking for love. I'm telling you, she'll fatten your pockets. She

6

might be a challenge because her brothers are protective, but I got a plan that will shut them down. Just hear me out." Blaze turned to his uncle but then thought about all his other schemes and waved him off.

"I ain't got time for your shit, Uncle Red. Get the fuck outta here."

"Alright, maybe you ain't got what it takes to bag her anyway." Blaze stopped in his tracks. He screwed up his face, pounded on his chest and spat.

"Niggah, do you see who the fuck you talking to?"

"I thought I did, that's why I came to you, but if you ain't up to the challenge...," Red had him hooked.

"Spit it!" Blaze was up for anything anyone threw his way. If it deemed to be bullshit he threw it in the wind.

"First things first." Uncle Red smiled victoriously, holding his hand out. "...the money."

Blaze huffed and dug in his pockets. He handed Red a wad of cash and waited for the details. Red grinned and held on tight to the cash, "Her name is...'

The time had finally come for Ritza to meet the love of her life. She would walk through fire to leave her old life behind. She wanted to feel secure, loved, and, most of all she wanted to live the glamorous life at any cost. She ran into a young man who caught her eye. She thanked Red for sending her to the store that day. God finally heard her prayers. She longed to be freed from the havoc going on in her house. She was young but not green. The only thing green about her was the dollar bill signs in her eyes.

"Hey Baby girl! You need me to help you?" Blaze moved in for the kill, flashing his irresistible smile.

"That's okay, I'm good." She made sure her backside was in full view.

"I can see." Blaze grinned like the Grinch about to steal Christmas as he scanned Ritza up and down stopping at her ass. "All good."

Yeah I can make tons of paper off this young honey, he thought. Blaze's bottom bitch detected Blaze's attention on someone else. She strutted over to Blaze. "Daddy, are you ready, Cinnamon called, she's needs to be picked up."

Blaze turned around with fire in his eyes. He started to raise his hand to smack the envy out of her mouth, but hesitated not wanting to scare off Ritza. Instead he shooed her off. "Girl, don't you see me talking to this beautiful lady. Step back." He never took his eyes off of

Ritza but his tone made his bottom bitch bite the top of her lip in pure horror. "Now back to you, beautiful."

"My name is Ritza." She laughed at the name the other woman called him. "Got that...*Daddy*."

Blaze didn't care for her sarcasm but let it slide. He had bigger fish to fry. "Since we have everything established, I'd like to get to know you. Can I get your number?"

Ritza thought about what to tell him. Red would skin her alive and so would her brothers if she even thought about talking to a man like Blaze. She didn't even have a number to give. "Well Baby girl?"

"Got paper?" she asked.

"Always," Blaze pulled out a wad of hundreds, peeled off a few and handed them to Ritza. She froze on the spot. She'd never had so much money in her hand at one time. Blaze stared at her. Ritza took it as a test and stared back at him, not knowing what to do with it.

"No silly...to write down your number," Blazed laughed at her naivety. Blaze's bottom bitch came back over to them. "I am so sorry Daddy, but Cinnamon and Candy are ready. They said they don't feel safe waiting with your money." The mere mention of money saved his bottom bitch from getting the shit beat out of her. She was pressing her luck.

"Start the car," he said without turning to look at her. She huffed and walked off. Ritza rolled her eyes at the interruption and tried to hand Blaze his money.

"No Baby girl, keep the money; it's for you and write your number here." Blaze opened his button up shirt revealing his smooth chocolate chest. "I want to keep it close to my heart." Ritza leaned in and wrote a number. "What's that?"

"My number. If I can't be #1 then I won't be anything." She tried to hand him back his money again, but Blaze refused.

"Okay Ritza. I gotchoo. I will meet up with you again, and next time I will step my game up. I know you're not the average beauty."

Ritza wanted to give him a way to reach her. He'd refuse taking back the money because if he did he would be playing himself, showing defeat. He didn't strike her as the type to be played. "So you know, huh?"

"Yeah Ritza, I know, I know."

Blaze walked off, leaving Ritza in awe. While Ritza waited for him to pull off, a block hugger named Chi approached. She instantly recognized him from walking with her brother to cop piff for Red.

"Ain't you Roz's little girl? You are too young to be checking for Blaze. He's out of your league." Ritza was insulted.

"I don't play in leagues...I play ballers." She flashed her money and walked back into the store to purchase a cell phone. Now she had a number to give him next time. Ritza was no dummy. She watched how her mother used what her momma gave her to get what she wanted and she would continue the cycle.

TRUST NO ONE

Ritza never told anyone about the money; not even her siblings. She slept with it stuffed in her panties for safekeeping. It seemed selfish, but she deserved every penny and was her only way out. Gradually as the days passed Ritza snuck in time after school so she could shop as much as possible without being noticed that her book bag was filled with new clothes and sneakers. Spending as much money as she did without thinking about her sister wasn't a smart move, but she couldn't stop herself after buying the first outfit and her very first pair of Air Jordans. She tried on the first outfit, and began dancing and prancing in front of the mirror as if she was on the runway. She felt like a million dollars in her two hundred dollar outfit.

"What trick? I look better than your raggedy ass. Yes, my man takes good care of me," Ritza giggled as she spoke into the dressing room mirror. Power came with those words. She'd been taunted and laughed at all her life, and now it was her turn to do the laughing.

Over the next few weeks Ritza hid quite a bit of clothes in the back of her closet. Each time she purchased a few items she would use the mall's bathroom to situate her bag. Before she realized it, all her books and gym clothes were thrown inti the trash. She replaced her future with all of the items she'd purchased, folding each piece of clothing as compact as allowed, to make everything fit.

Red was standing at the door when she came home. "Where the hell have you been? Your brothers waited for you at the school and the only one standing there was Fallon...crying!"

Ritza lowered her head. She had forgotten all about her younger sister Fallon, and she'd do this more than once. "Red, I told you and Momma last night I had a special project to do for science class at the library." Ritza lied.

Red couldn't tell if she was telling the truth or not. His drunken state kept him from remembering anything. She'd never lied to him before, so he gave her the benefit of the doubt. "Take your butt in your room and get ready for school tomorrow. Wash your sister up, and then get out here and get dinner started. I ain't bought groceries this week for nothing. Me and yo momma got some things to do so don't none of y'all even think about knocking on that bedroom door."

Red cut his eyes at Ritza checking out how much she blossomed since he last talked to Blaze. He shook his head remembering about his promise. He felt a twinge of guilt about selling her soul to the devil. He had grown to like Ritza the most. She rarely complained about anything, kept good grades and took care of her siblings like their momma used to, but if he didn't make good on his promise to Blaze he knew death would find him, uncle or not. He regretted putting Ritza in harm's way and now he had to think of a way to keep her safe from Blaze.

After putting Fallon in the tub, Ritza went back to her room. She retrieved her duffle bag and crawled to the back of her closet. It was her getaway and her hidden spot for her new wardrobe. She pulled out a garbage bag used to stuff a large hole to keep out the rats, and placed the new clothes and sneakers she got earlier into the hole.

"There! Now all I have to do is figure out how I am going to wear them to school."

The thought of Blaze getting hold of Ritza's innocence began to sicken Red. For the first in a long time Red had a conscious. Blaze violating Ritza combined with not working, consumed him. He began numbing his worries with his addiction every time he made a dime. At one time he helped Roz with her household expenses, but when he couldn't keep up, he stayed out later getting high more and more. He had to see what he could do to work off his debt to his nephew.

Red summed up the courage when he confronted his nephew. "Look Blaze, I need to talk to you about my proposal."

"Spit it out Red. Time is money and I don't have time to give."

11

Red took off his hat and started twisting it with his hands as if he was ringing out the sweat. "Ritza's a good girl, Blaze. I thought about our deal long and hard, and she ain't cut out for what you have in store for her. Let me work out something else with you. She's going places, man and she's had a tough life."

Blaze grinned, "What? I know you ain't grown a fucking conscious? You ain't had a problem when I laced your greedy fucking pockets with my bread!"

Red stepped back as he spoke. "I...I..."

Blaze's eyes were dark as coal for a second he thought he saw the image of Lucifer himself in them. When Blaze spoke Red lowered his head. "You must be stuck on stupid, niggah. Nah, a bitch like Ritza is a dime piece fo' sho'! I already invested in her. The game is in motion. Can't help you, partnah!"

Red wiped the sweat forming on his brow. "What? When? When did you run into Ritza?"

"Man, don't fool with me. I know you sent her to the store so I would get a glimpse of what I will be working with, or shall I say, what she will be working with for me. I hit her off with about six hundred to get her juices running. You can't afford the debt...six hundred on top of the three G's I fronted you?"

"I will pay you every week 'til you're paid in full. Just leave Ritza alone."

Blaze laughed at his proposition, "Unc' you must be on that shit hard. What the fuck you think this is? You want a fuckin' payment plan?" Blaze shook his head and laughed. "I ain't trying to give her up. What's done is done, 'til death do us part." Blaze's sinister laugh sent chills up Red's spine lifting the hairs on the back of his neck.

Red reached out for Blaze's arm to give one more plea. Blaze smacked him with the back of his hand. "Don't you ever touch me! I'll kill yo' ass the next time you fucking touch me. Fam or not, feel me?" Blaze dusted off his arm. The mere thought of Red touching him felt like it left a film of dirt.

Insulted by his nephew's blatant disrespect, Red walked away mumbling, "It's like that, nephew? Humph, be careful what you pray for."

What's up with Red? He's acting like I'm a damn prisoner. I ain't been able to run into Blaze, or nothing. Every time I ask him can I leave the house alone, he yells NO! Calling me names and shit. Fuck that niggah, he ain't my daddy.

THE FLIP SIDE OF THE GAME

Ritza needed to be free, she needed to taste the streets, and Red kept her from the one thing she needed most, Blaze. She couldn't take it and decided to scheme her way out. She was watching and growing wiser each day. Blaze was giving her more and more each day but she never slept that all this was play for her play.

"Excuse me; I wanted you to know I started my job at the library." Ritza was meeting Blaze.

Roz looked lost. She didn't know Ritza had money. Before Roz said okay, Red answered Ritza instead, "Fine. If that is what you are claiming but, if you ain't there... you already know." Red tugged on his belt.

Ritza huffed, but she had a plan already in motion. She already figured he wouldn't fully believe her. Ritza tossed and turned most of the night. The anticipation of seeing Blaze made her eager. All she thought about was getting more money from him. She looked over at her alarm clock; 4am. Ritza scooted out of bed, trying not to awaken Fallon. She climbed to the back of her closet to retrieve a new outfit and the Jordan's she bought and hurriedly placed them in her duffle bag. She spent the rest of her time selecting something for Fallon to wear and doing her hair. She thanked God they both inherited a fine grade of hair from their absent father. She flat twisted the front and pinned up the back in a hair clip.

Red had been up all night from getting high when he noticed a light creeping out from under her bedroom door. He knocked on the door to find Ritza talking to herself in the mirror.

"Yes, Daddy, I need some money to get my hair done."

Red shook his head; he knew she was already hooked, "Girl, what the hell are you doing up? Who you calling, Daddy?"

Ritza jumped, "Uh, morning Red. I'm practicing on how to ask my father for a few dollars to get my hair done."

"Since when you been talking to yo' *daddy?*"

Ritza lowered her head as she spoke, "I ain't been. That's why I'm practicing."

Red didn't say another word. How could he? He closed the door and left her standing at the mirror.

TRUE TO THE GAME

On the way to school, Ritza was exceptionally happy. She had been rushing them all morning.

"Why are you so happy about going to school?"

Ritza smiled, keeping her secret. Fallon whined at the fast pace Ritza made her walk. "Slow down. I can't keep up."

"Girl, don't you want to get there early for breakfast. I think they're having those French toast sticks you like."

Fallon's whining stopped and she sped up her pace. "Oh yeah, Red said you have to sit with me at the library so you can both hang up playing basketball after school," Ritza began to set her plan in motion.

Troy cursed, followed by Dante. "Ain't nobody wanna sit at the library all day. We ain't got time fa' dat! We got a game against these two suckers for that bread." Her brothers looked at each other and nodded.

Ritza scolded them, "I'mma tell Red. He said..."

"Look, how about we give you some if you let us drop you and Fallon off and pick y'all up after we finish. Red ain't gotta know shit."

Ritza had them where she wanted them, and to seal the deal, added, "Yea, okay. You right. He ain't our Daddy."

Her brothers hugged her and agreed, "Sure aint."

Now, all she had to do was find a way to bribe Fallon not to squeal.

Ritza was never too fancy about having friends. She always stayed secluded. It lessened her chances of being in the center of attention. However, today she wished she had one person she could share her secret with, and to sit with Fallon while she went on her "Get Money" mission.

Right now, the mission seemed impossible. Fallon clung to her everywhere they went and today was no different. Her sister also shied away from mingling with the other children. Soon as Ritza hit school grounds, she rushed Fallon to the cafeteria and ran to the girl's bathroom. She did not want any of her classmates to recognize that she had changed her clothes. She sang in the bathroom stall as she got dressed "She's got her own! Independent queen..."

Ritza was singing so loud she never heard the door swing open and shut. She just kept singing that same verse to Jamie Fox's song Independent Woman. "She's got her own!" It was the first time in her life she didn't have on Hand Me Downs.

She opened the stall door, and was hit with laughter from a few of the girls in her class. They were now laughing in her face, Ritza was standing in the new with her hands on her hips.

"Oh shit! Ritza done borrowed somebody's shit," one said.

"It ain't even the first of the month," the second one said then balled over holding her stomach and burst out in laughter.

The last girl noticed that when Ritza dressed up, she was truly pretty. So you know, envy and jealousy kicked in. "She's still dirty; bet she didn't even wash her ass. Talking about she has her own. Really Ritza? You, you got your own?"

Ritza didn't break a sweat when she threw her hair over her shoulder dropped one hand from her hip and popped one leg back. "Nah, you right, I ain't got my own."

The last girl nodded to her friends. "Just like I thought, she's a borrowing bitch. Where they do that at? One Broke Bitch Drive?"

Ritza let out a sigh then she hit them below the belt with sarcasm, "I ain't got my own, but I am *independent.*"

"Girl, that don't make sense. You must ain't listening to the words right. And she's stupid!"

"Damn, girl you are right again. I'm *in* my man's pocket and it *depend*s which day of the week I decide to put a *dent* in his wallet. Now, if you will excuse me BITCHES, I ain't got time for haters."

Ritza walked past them and before she exited she turned around and said, "Bye haters, this is just the beginning!" They were so stunned by her actions before they could retaliate, she was gone.

All day the boys flocked around Ritza, and she reveled in all the attention. She developed beefs that she gladly accepted. For the first time in her life, she was the center of attention and she liked it. She knew she had to see Blaze. There was no way she was going back to the old Ritza. She wanted to boast like Lauren London who played in the movie ATL. She wanted to always rock the new, new shit! She didn't care what she had to do to get that paper, she was never going back to having nothing! The bell rang to close out the school day and Ritza rushed to change her clothes and then to get Fallon.

PIMP

"Ritza, slow down."

Ritza ignored her and helped Fallon with her book bag before pulling her arm and nearly dragging her down the school steps two at a time. The library was packed with kids from the neighborhood whose parents couldn't afford daycare. Ritza asked the librarian about what activities were going on for the younger children. She was ecstatic to find out that story reading would be starting in five minutes and that it would last two hours. She signed Fallon up, told her she'd be back to get her, redressed, and headed a few blocks down to the "spot" to find Blaze. All the dressing and redressing was time consuming but it's what she had to do, for now.

Once Ritza was in an eye and ear shot of Blaze, she paid close attention to the atmosphere. She didn't want to take a chance running into Red, or anyone who could report that she wasn't at the library. She didn't expect all that was revealed to her on this day. She knew Blaze was a dealer, but the cards he was shuffling didn't come in brown paper bags. Ritza leaned up against the bus stop sign trying to remain inconspicuous. She watched as Blaze scream and yell at the woman that interrupted their conversation the other day. He paced back and forth, swinging his arms wildly as he spoke.

18

"Bitch, have you lost your fucking mind? If I say, fuck that niggah that's what you do! Now find out where that niggah is, so I can drop your ass off." The woman lowered her head and apologized. "I thought so. You gonna make my money bitch, fo' I drop your ass right here."

The woman nodded as she got into the car.

"This dude is a *pimp*?" Ritza gasped and placed her hand over her mouth. "I know his ass ain't trying to put me out there like no slab!" To Ritza there was a difference from having hoes than **having** hoes.

Before Blaze pulled off, Ritza called out his name. Blaze heard money ringing in his ears. He spotted Ritza then waved for her to come. "Hey, Shorty. You're looking good, Lil mama." Blaze knew she was a diamond in the rough. He looked her up and down and nodded. The shit a little cold cash does for a sistah. "So, what up? I see you've been putting that change I gave you to good use. *Damn, good use.*"

Ritza twisted up her lip. "Is that your way of *complimenting* a young lady?"

Blaze laughed, "Nah Ma, you look beautiful."

Ritza went into her stance. "That's better. So, what are you up to?"

Blaze got out of the car and sat on the hood. He wasn't your Don Juan looking pimp. He didn't wear gators or a flamboyant suit holding a pimp cup like the pimps Ritza saw on T.V. or in music videos. He was your modern day street hustler type pimp. His hair was faded into a Caesar and his neck was adorned by one long chain studded out in red and orange diamonds that carried a charm that read BLAZE with flames. She wasn't sure what the name of his jeans were, but she'd seen them before on the street hustlers. His gear was meant to scream BOSS and it did.

"So, can I get your number now?"

"I don't think you have shown me that I am your number one. You're still with that chic." Ritza pointed to the woman in the car who wouldn't stop rolling her eyes.

"Girl, that ain't nothing but business. I want you to be pleasure. I got her on my chain, but I want you on my arm. I'm really feeling you."

Ritza wasn't buying it. "Business, huh?" Ritza stared at the woman's jewelry and her expensive pocketbook and attire. "I see she's rockin' Gucci. You put a lot into your business."

"Baby you gotta spend money to make money," was all Blaze said. But he was thinking that this young girl ain't as green as he thought.

19

"What do you do for pleasure?" Blaze questioned, getting to the point. He watched her body language and how she seemed to be thinking about what to say before she spoke.

I kind of like her game. She's bound to squeeze niggah's pockets like fresh orange juice, he thought.

"So you want Prada, if she's rocking Gucci? I gotchoo ma," Blaze dug into his pockets and pulled out what seemed like enough money to choke a horse, and peeled off several bills and handed it to Ritza. This time he counted it out, "One thousand...five. Is that good for today?"

Ritza didn't want to seem stunned. "I guess. I just want you to know you can't buy me. I want to spend some time with you too." Watching reality shows seemed to be paying off for Ritza. Everything she said was rehearsed and calculated. *This type of shit does happen in real life.*

"Will do, Love. Check me at this same spot tomorrow morning at eight. We can hit the city and really do some shopping."

Ritza didn't know how to respond. There was no way she could get away with missing school. Now her plan didn't seem to be so calculated. *I'mma have to stay home sick tomorrow. When Red and ma go to work I can be out.* She began to plot in her head as she stared at Blaze's pretty mouth.

"I know you have school, so I'll have you back by the time it lets out. I don't want your momma all up in my shit. So, don't worry."

Ritza decided to lay her shit on the line. She didn't want him to think she could just up and go with him whenever he asks. "Look Blaze, you know I ain't even supposed to be talking to you. My momma would kill me if she even knew, let alone skipping school. My stepfather has me on lock down. Do you know what I had to do to hide the shit I'd been buying? How are we going to do this cause I don't want to disappoint my mama?"

Blaze knew this obstacle would come. Red warned him it would before he got soft. Ritza was a good girl. "I like that you put it out there like that. We'll think of something. Just keep doing what you're doing and everything will fall into place."

Ritza shook her head. "Okay, but don't be surprised when I tell you my mama done kicked my ass out."

Blaze smiled, "If that happens Ma, I'll take full responsibility. I said I gotchoo, remember. Now, let me roll out, business is calling. If you want me to be able to treat you right, I gotta make this money."

He leaned in and kissed Ritza on the lips. She stood frozen with her mouth slightly open. It was her first kiss.

ME AND MY BOYFRIEND

From that day, they were inseparable. She did skip school that next day, and damn near every day after that. Ritza was hooked on a drug named Blaze. She fought repeatedly with her mother about her missing school and asking where she was getting the new clothes. Ritza even bought her sister and brothers clothing, and sneakers. The final straw was when Ritza's mother fought her and gave her a black eye for coming in the house after dark.

"You think your ass is grown? Sluttin' around in those streets, doing God knows fuckin' what. If you can't respect this house, your ass has got to go." Roz's words pierced her soul.

Slut? Ritza was still a virgin. Blaze didn't treat Ritza like he did the others. He was taking his time grooming her. He even told her he wanted to get to know her, and didn't want to pressure her.

"You can think what you want Ma, but I aint no ho'. I ain't never even had sex. Everybody doesn't trick to get what they want like... " That was where the slap came in. "I'm outah here!" Ritza screamed, holding her cheek. "You're a fuckin' trip!" Then came the left hook that sent Ritza falling on her ass. Ritza stood. Her first thought was to stomp a mud whole in her mother's ass but then Fallon ran over to her sister and held on to her waist for dear life.

22

Ritza's look of horror on her face matched Fallon's. Their oldest brother left home and had enlisted in the army; and Dante was roaming the streets, rarely ever coming home. Fallon knew she would be left at home alone and at times in the cold alone and hungry. She also knew once Ritza left, she would never come back.

"Ritza please stay. I don't want you to go. I will be alone, when mama..." Roz glared at Fallon.

"When I what, Fallon?"

Fallon cried. "When you get..."

"Shut up Fallon and go to your room!"

Fallon looked up at Ritza with pleading, watery eyes. Ritza looked away. "Now Fallon!" Her lil sister did as her mother told her to. Not all respect was gone for her mother. Ritza soon followed her to their room. As she stuffed her belonging in her bags, she spoke to Fallon.

"Baby sis, I will be back for you. I'mma take you out of here as soon as I get a place. I promise."

Fallon looked Ritza in her eyes, "You promise?"

Ritza hugged her sister but before she left made her first mistake. "I promise."

CHILD OF A CRACKHEAD

Roz was a full blown suck a dick for a dollar and fifteen cents crack head now. Red turned her out. Roz sat on the sofa counting what was left of her unemployment check repeatedly. It would be the last one she received. She applied for cash assistance from the welfare, but was denied because she received unemployment. Roz received forty-five dollars in food stamps all of which was minutes after she received them. She sat at the table staring into her own world. Her elbows were planted on the stained table cloth as she dragged hard on her Newport. She reminisced about the night she took her first hit.

"Roz come on in the room, I got something for you." Roz remembered Red's thunderous voice.

She remembered jumping up from the couch and stuffed her money she about to hand Fallon, back in her pocket. Fallon smiled hoping that she'd work her magic (as Roz called it) on Red to get her a meal. Fallon sat on the worn out sofa and patiently waited.

Roz entered the smoke filled room. Red was lying across the bed in his work clothes. Roz cupped her hands over her face covering her mouth and nose in unison.

"Red, what the hell you smoking in here? That shit stinks."

"It may stink but, it's damn good."

24

Roz noticed a small rock-like substance on her good china plate. There was a mound of weed next to it.

"Come hit this, Roz."

Roz knew Red was on something. He was the nicest person one minute and an asshole the next.

"Red, I ain't got time for that. I'm trying to figure out how I'm going to feed my baby. You got a few dollars to spare?" Roz went into action. She swayed her hips and sucked on the tip of her finger.

"That shit aint gonna work tonight, Roz. This high is far greater than that sloppy pussy you got. Now, if you come over here, and hit this with me. I'll give Fallon a few dollars to walk to the corner store to get some spiced ham and cheese."

Roz's eyes lit up. Her main concern was Fallon since Dante and Ritza were now out of the house. Roz sat on the edge of the bed and smoked a blunt with Red. When she took the first hit, she understood why Red refused her pussy. The high was like no other. She had smoked weed before, but this was different. She laid fback and leaned against the headboard. Her mind seemed to be free of all the headaches about money, being unemployed and her child's needs. It was all about her and the dark green rolled paper she was holding. After a few hours of smoking with Red, it was all she cared about from then on. Fallon never got the money for the lunchmeat.

TWO TEARS IN A BUCKET

Ritza could hear her mother saying that men make promises and believe that they can be broken. It was all part of their game. She hoped that was not the case. She dropped her bags at her feet and took a deep breath. The home was beautiful. She looked at the address and up at the number on the partial brick wall in front of the home. Surprised at its splendor, she rang the bell and waited.

It didn't take long for one of his ho's to come to the door. She screwed her face and rolled her eyes never moving out of the way to allow Ritza to enter. So Ritza pushed past her calling out Blaze's name.

"Blaze

Trying not to admire his home, Ritza walked through the foyer stopping at the beginning of the staircase. Cinnamon followed behind her wrapped in a long see through gown. With her arms crossed. Things were definitely going to change when she saw Ritza standing on the porch like a lost puppy.

"Whatchoo want with Blaze? Ain't you too young to be out this late? You ain't but 13, right?"

Ritza understood she felt threatened. She was half her age and looking to move in.

"Look, I ain't here to step on your toes. What you are to Blaze is nothing like what I am trying to be. So, no threat here. Keep doing

26

what you're doing. Make that money. Do you." Ritza tried to give Cinnamon dap but Cinnamon failed to find the humor in her naivety.

"You have a lot to learn. You think Blaze..."

"Somebody got my name slipping off their tongue?" Cinnamon's eyes widened her mouth remained shaped for words as she struggled to explain.

"Well I was coming downstairs to get the Moscato for...uh...I mean I heard the bell and it was...well the bell rang and Reesa, I mean Ritza..."

Blaze was standing at the top of the staircase looking over the banister.

"Girl, shut the hell up and goodnight! You need your beauty sleep. Aint nothing worse than an ugly tired looking ho. First, show my wifey to the entertainment room." Cinnamon knew the game he was preparing to put Ritza through.

In a sense she wanted to whisper to her, "RUN!!! RUN!!!! And don't look back. He's gonna kill your dreams and pimp you like the rest of us." But she knew that it would be the death of her. "Yes, Blaze!"

Blaze smiled down at Ritza. "I'm going to put on something more appropriate, give me a sec." Ritza was reluctant when she saw his bare chest with a pair of boxer drawers on. She had a change of heart when he excused himself.

Cinnamon took her into the entertainment room and offered her a soda. "I would have offered you something stronger but you are just a baby, I mean young lady."

Ritza laughed. "I got more sense than that, age has nothing to do with it. Maybe you need to learn how to just say no." Cinnamon's smile was sincere whether Ritza knew it or not. Blaze had his work cut out for him. This one was no one's follower.

"Whatever." Cinnamon walked out of the room leaving Ritza alone to admire the décor. There were 3, 60' inch plasma television one had a game console hooked up to it the other a DVD player and surround sound and the other a cable box and a keyboard sat on top.

She was amazed by the popcorn machine on one side of the room and 8 fluffy leather reclining chairs lined up theater style. He really had a movie theater popcorn maker. And a glass case with all sorts of movie show candy, posters of all the Madea movies and a picture of him and Tyler Perry rested on the wall. She was definitely impressed.

All of this was tucked away in a cul-de-sac on the north end of Bridgeport.

"So, who do I have to thank for this visit?"

Ritza sat on the sofa looking into her lap. When she first approached his home she had all the nerve she needed but with him now in her presence she didn't know how to tell him she was moving in. Blaze sat next to her, his arm across the top of the couch. He was so close she could smell his minty fresh breath.

"I saw you had some luggage in my foyer? You staying awhile?" Ritza nodded. "Look Ritza, you are my girl and..."

Ritza jumped up from the sofa placed her hands on her hips and popped her neck back. "What's up with this lil girl talk? What's that make you? I am not a little girl, or your girl? If I am going to be your lady you are going to stop disrespecting me. That goes for your bottom feeders too." The more Ritza demanded the bigger the vain on the side of Blaze's neck got. He was not use to a female jumping in his face. He reached out for her talking hands and pulled her back own on the couch.

"Ritza, you have to let a man be the man. You can put down your guard. I am here to love you, not fight you. I am here to respect you as the beautiful young woman you are not the older woman you're not. Never be ashamed of your age and what you don't know. Never fake it to you make it. Listen, watch and learn. And most of all stick school out and read, read, read. Ain't nothing worse than a know it all, don't know nothing, dumb, grown acting chick. Never think people can't see through a façade."

Ritza listened intensively. "A façade?"

"Yea baby, meaning people can see when you are faking; perpetrating. Feel me? So be you at all times. If you are ashamed of you then polish the real you until it shines." Ritza and Blaze talked all night. He was spitting jewels on her that she would learn to wear in some of the worse situations. It was close to 2am when Ritza's stomach started growling. "Hungry much?"

Instead of being defensive she laughed and he joined in. Cinnamon never left the doorway. She listened the entire time. "Damn, he's getting better. I didn't think she'd melt so fast." When she hurt footsteps she darted up the staircase.

"Let me show you the place and where you will be sleeping. First thing first; the kitchen." Blaze growled, teasing Ritza about her stomach crying out in hunger. "Oh, you got jokes for days."

Blaze had the bomb skills in the kitchen. He whipped up some pasta, garlic bread and gave her an orange Crush to wash it down. The tour of the house kept Ritza wanting to live this lifestyle. She would have never guessed that street hugger like Blaze would have a library of street lit. Blaze pulled a book off the shelf called Fornication by Julia Press Simmons.

"Here Ritza read this. I guarantee you will look at life differently. Its late lets go to bed. We can take care of everything else that needs to be done after you come from school."

"School?"

Blaze's face was now serious. "Yes, school."

Blaze lead Ritza upstairs. She hadn't that much attention and she loved every minute and every second of it. "I know you are going to love this bed." Blaze opened the door to the biggest and prettiest bedroom Ritza ever saw and it showed on her face.

"Wow! This is...this is..." Ritza sat on the bed and then patted the space beside her. What she did not understand was Blazes response. He never left the doorway. He stood there smiling but shaking his head no.

"Baby girl, you are still a minor. I don't get down like that. We are gonna keep this right till the time is right. You need to be ready. I am a

29

very experienced man and I need you to understand when the time comes it will be the right time...on your time. Come give me kiss." Ritza slid off the bed of knowing if she should be hurt or glad he respects her. She stood in front of Blaze not knowing what to do. This would be her 2nd kiss. Blaze leaned in and she closed her eyes. The peck he gave her at first made her want more. So she pulled him closer and he landed another kiss holding her face moving her hair from her face. First it was soft then she felt a sweet delicate pressure. They were short kisses and then the time span lengthened. His hands left her face and rested on her lower backside as he slightly lifted her closer to him. The feeling of his warm tongue slowly tangled with her tongue teaching her but yet not taking away from the euphoric feeling.

His touch was so mesmerizing Ritza felt light on her feet. She let every muscle in her back go and fell limp in his arms. His hand seem to have been everywhere. When he moved his hands from her back to her ass she could still feel them in both places. She was getting tingles in places she never knew existed.

Half understanding what was happening to her she wet herself; so she thought. Embarrassed by her wetness she pushed him back and out of the doorway. He smiled, tapped her on the tip of her nose and said goodnight.

When she heard his steps get further away she held her heart. "Slow your roll Ritzy...he's just a man....just a man. All players have game." She listened to her brother try to throw game to girls all the time. Even Red, he thought he had game too. The only difference, Blaze had a ball of flaming fire with his game and spoke the language of a true pimp!

She knew it was all game. She read enough books and watched enough television to know that men wooed their way in, but a true man keeps wooing. "We'll see if I am separate from the rest."

Ritza was feeling less than clean and wanted to take a shower. She undressed took out her old bathrobe and wrapped her body up. She felt out of place compared to the nightgown and robe Cinnamon wore. It was kiddie; Pretty Kitty slippers to match. Ritza walked the hall not knowing which room was whose. She walked up to the first door and placed her ear to it. Moans and groans were faint but consistent. "Someone is getting it on and poppin'."

Ritza covered her mouth and giggled. She wondered if who it was. Not wanting to intrude she moved to the next door which was slightly ajar. She could not believe what she saw. Cinnamon's ass was perched in the air with her knees planted between someone else's knees and her face buried between their legs. Even though Ritza gasped she doubted Cinnamon heard anything above all the slurping and sucking. Ritza was sort of turned on by the act, the body movement, the sexual tunes and howling lyrics that were being shared. Cinnamon's ass moved in a circular motion. Her speed was parallel with the moans and groans as if it served as a guide. Ritza was so engulfed in the act she too was moving her neck with the rhythm. She was startled when the melodic moans turned into hard grunts then a loud scream. Ritza leaned back making sure she was not seen. When the moaning began again Ritza found herself tempted to watch. This time finding comfort by leaning her head and body along the frame of the door. Cinnamon was on the bottom but yet still was on her knees, back relaxed but ass still poked into the crotch of the giver. The frame seemed smaller now that the giver was curved over Cinnamon's slender body; almost glued to her frame. The giver was the color of mocha pudding, the long shaft...and when I say long I mean extra-long and deep chocolate. It was oddly mismatched compared to the rest of the giver. The color was easily noticed because of the distance between their bodies. Almost equally odd, the face of the giver; was almost pretty; eyebrows defined; thinly arched with a honey blond colored; hair close cut, sort of faded. It too was blonde and highlighted, with shades of warm browns.

When Cinnamon moaned with sheer delight Ritza's lips parted slowly, almost moaning with her. Their bodies moved like they were speaking to each other telling each other stories, whispering secrets on just when to move and in what direction. Cinnamon then positioned her fingers as if holding herself, moving them in a sort of rubbing motion. That's when the moans grew more intense than like the last time. Cinnamon's partner leaned off of her and roared like Tarzan and that's when Ritza's cover was blown.

"AHHHH SHIT!" Ritza couldn't contain herself. She couldn't move; fixated on the boobs and erect nipples of Cinnamon's partner. She mumbled under her breath still confused. "He's a she? But how, she has a ...."

The bedmates looked at Ritza and laughed. "Who's the dumb chick? One of my brother's new bitches?" As she spoke she crawled off the bed and detached her 9-inch and simply plopped on the end of the bed, blowing Ritza's mind. After the initial shock it dawned on her that the person she thought was a guy was indeed lesbian stud. The

31

stud blew her a kiss and startled Ritza. "Fuck that!" Ritza turned and bolted to her room locking the door behind her. "Ewww! Cinnamon was eating..."

REAL BITCHES DO REAL THINGS

Ritza was getting dressed for the day. She laid her clothes out like she did every Saturday since Blaze was lacing her pockets. Her Vickies bra and matching boy shorts enhanced her young frame. During the night Ritza 's cell phone was on the edge of the bed. She gave Fallon the number to call; when she needed to talk. Now she was following the low toned ring. She bent over to lift the bed skirt and the door opened. "Damn baby! 13 years old and got all that in the trunk. Oh yea...he can pick 'em"

Ritza stood quickly. She knew exactly who just invaded her privacy, but what could she say. "Damn baby nothing, yes he can pick 'em and no I am not 13 but rightly tight." Ritza had quick wit. She licked the tip of her pointer finger and drew a line in mid-air. "Hmmph...one for me...none for you; little boy blue...and by the way just for your information, I am strictly dickly." She stepped back.

"Touché lil mama." Ritza screwed her face up. "Meaning you got me...you're right. The name is Odessa. I am Byron's sister."

"Okay and..."Ritza wondered why Odessa was even in her room.

Odessa noticed the confused look on Ritza's face. "I'm sorry, Byron is Blaze's real name." Ritza lightened up. She didn't want beef in the family already.

"So, where is my baby?"

33

Odessa shook her head at Ritza putting that label on her brother. This girl is all mouth because she aint the shiniest Apple Bottom. Odessa dug in her pocket and pulled out a roll of money and tossed it top Ritza.

"Me?"

"Yeah. He said go shopping. Get rid of that at the playground look." Ritza looked at her outfit for the day. Her new "J's True Religions and a Banana Republic pullover was a bit hood and young'nish. "You got twenty minutes. I aint got all day."

Odessa wasn't bad company. It was the first time Ritza ever told anyone about her childhood. No one ever knew about her mother and what she made her and her siblings do when she got high. "Damn Riz, in the cold? You better thank God for that car. And I thought I had it bad. Where is your sis now?"

Ritza's whole demeanor changed. None of this was new to Odessa. She'd heard it all before; stories far worse. She was the walking diary; confession booth for all Blaze's tricks. It served two purposes. When she sympathized it got her the best emotional sex and Blaze the information he needed. "I had to leave her with my mom. Don't get me wrong my mom will look out for her the best as she can. I'll have to find a way to get them both away from Red." Odessa made a mental note of everything Ritza told her. Odessa shifted the car gears in park and took a deep breath and exhaled.

"Sorry I ruined your mood. Let's drop your past and work on your future with my brother. Come on bum-bitch. First stop, Gucci." Ritza playfully shoved Odessa.

"Ok, Rug Muncher. Let's do this!" Odessa had to laugh at the young girl's humor.

TEMPTING HER

"**A**wwww ain't that a sob story! Come on Dessa, we've heard it all before. I can't let your softness for pussy fuck wid my money. I told you to stop showing sympathy for every stray I bring up in here. This is business. Remember that! Now, where's my money?"

Odessa shook her head and dug out her earnings. She knew he was a cold son of a bitch, but dang. She truly thought he liked shorty. She hesitated on telling him about her sister but knew if she didn't tell him and he found out that she knew his promise to her would be broken.

Odessa had an obligation to her brother. She did whatever was asked of her. Turn a trick; the treats on her. Keep his girls in check; check! There was no line should would not cross for Blaze. She even copped to a drug and gun charge just to make sure he kept his word. Blaze was a true believer that a man is nothing without his wallet and his word. But if someone ever crossed him and picked his wallet or didn't keep up with their obligation to him everything he promised was a thing of the past. Odessa needed him to take good care of her son's medical expenses. He had special needs. And only Blaze had that resource and funds on that level. She had to fess up even though something told her that it would've been more valuable kept.

35

"You know she has a sister right? Suppose to be fine and tender like shawty" Blaze said nothing but don't think for once his mind was not in play. He made a mental note to send his strong, Scar to check Red to see why he was holding out.

Without knocking Ritza barged in on Odessa and Blaze talking. She rushed into Blaze's arm before he could chastise her on breaking his golden rule. "Knock before you enter. This is my shit!" She threw her arms around his neck practically wrapping her calves around his waist; hugging him with gratitude.

"Thank you baby for the shopping spree. I can't wait to show you my new look. After I go put on the finishing touches with Odessa tomorrow you will see this lil girl has upgraded to grown and sexy." Ritza was tickled. "Let me show you my new walk." Ritz turned around winked over her shoulder and then blew a kiss at Blaze. With ease Ritza strutted with the confidence of America's Top Model.

Odessa grinned. "Work it girl!"

Blaze was impressed. "Just for that display of sexiness. I am going to take you out on the town. My money has been kind of low so I am waiting on these bitches to get in with my bread. Bills are piling up and the help aint doing too much help. I gotta get some new bitches up in here to put in some work since I got me a real women on my arm." Blaze turned to Ritza who was blushing and feeling highly favored.

"I want to be able to keep you looking good. Soon you will be needing your own whip." Ritza's eyes widened. She jumped up and down grabbed Odessa under her arm. "Girl come on. I need to get fly for my man." Odessa peered at her. "I mean, I want to get ready for our night out. Can you help me get ready?" Ritza looked at her for approval. Odessa nodded. They walked past Blaze and he slipped Odessa a folded up bill for teaching Ritza. She shared more about her lil' sister.

Ritza gradually appreciated being around Odessa. She had someone to share her thoughts with. Her comfort ability allowed her to strip from her clothes talking pulling off piece by piece without feeling odd. "Was my walk good? Was I really sexy? What do you think I should wear? Did he say out on the town or out to eat?" She was down to her bare essentials. "I want to look good for Blaze?"

"Oh, that aint even gonna be a problem." Odessa shook her head. She knew what was in the making for Ritza tonight.

Not even an hour passed and Ritza transformed into a beautiful woman. Her black low cut dress revealed just enough cleavage to arouse and concealed enough to keep you wondering. Just above the knee gave it class but it hugged her every curve bringing out her grown and sexy appeal. Just the right accessories, just the right inched heals. Odessa had outdone herself. "You are rocking that dress, boo!" Ritza shied down bringing out her innocence.

"Really?"

The guilt kicked back in and Odessa became inpatient.

"Girl. Just come on. Don't know body want to hear his mouth. Fix your make-up and tighten up your head and let's go." Odessa had to kill her shine so that she was not too confident. Vulnerability and her eagerness to please Blaze was what Odessa banked on.

RIDE TO DIE CHIC

When Blaze heard heals click against the hardwoods floor drawing near he shoved Cinnamon on cue and started shouting. "Whatchoo mean your short. What about the rest of them? This is all you bring to me?" Blaze waved the small wad of money wildly. "I've got bills bitch and they ain't all mine. I keep y'all tight, looking good, Louie, Gucci, Coach, Minollo, Mike Korrs right? I keep you with the latest hairstyles. Ain't that wig you wearing now a thousand dollars? I pay for your mama's bills so that your bastard son can go to private school right?"

Then Blaze took it a step further exposing Odessa's secret to show he was serious on building his trick empire. He pointed to Odessa who was now entering the room. "And you, I pay for your sick son, right? I pay his hospital and therapy bills don't I?" Furious Odessa stormed out the room. "Not to mention the bills in here. Y'all must wanna be homeless. You trying to make me look bad in front of my new love. Trying to make me seem like some broke niggah that can't give her the world. I am falling for this girl and you're fucking up my plans for me to allow her to live like the queen she is. Fuck outtah here!" Cinnamon stood quiet with the other two bitches. "And you two are worthless. Next time you come up in this bitch without my fuckin' money its

38

going be some slow singing and flower bringing." Cinnamon made the grave mistake of speaking without being spoken to.

"It ain't they fault Daddy. Those parties you took us to wanted young girls; between teens."

Blaze's nose flared as he raised his hand and connected with Cinnamon's cheek. The sound echoed throughout the foyer; sending chills up Ritza's spine. "So, you blaming me? Bitch please, put some fucking ponytails and ribbons in your hair next the fuck time. Make it happen cause the next two events are gonna be the fucking same." Cinnamon sobbed as the other girls hid behind her.

"Dessa! Dessa!" Odessa came back in the room you could tell she was still fuming from Blaze's words. "Teach these dumb ass hoes to look like my baby before the make-over." Cinnamon spoke out of turn again as if the smack was not still stinging.

"She can't do ...." BAM!!!! Blaze hit her again and again and again. Ritza couldn't take any more. She rushed over to Blaze.

"Baby please. You're gonna kill her and then what good will that do. It ain't worth me loosing you." Blaze stopped with his hand in mid-air.

"OMG! I ain't want you to see this side of me. I don't want you to see me as some kind of man who fucks up his bitches. But I wanna be able to keep you, give you everything you ever wanted. I know you had a hard childhood. But with these old ass bitches bullshitting my money I feel they don't respect you or what I want do for you baby, you feel me?" That was the nicest thing anyone ever said to her and she was hooked on his dedication to make her happy. She wanted to give him the same.

Cinnamon was curled up on the floor holding her face crying uncontrollably. "Let me talk to her baby." Ritza attempted to pick Cinnamon up from the floor her girls rushed in to help. "Cinnamon, when you say the room was full of between teens what did you mean?"

Cinnamon explained. "Teenie boppers, like girls your age in catholic uniforms the whole nine. We looked like their mother's. We made money giving head but that's it. No one gives head like a seasoned bitch ya know?" Ritza nodded.

"So, they looked like me, you said?" Cinnamon nodded. "Ok, ya'll clean her up and let me talk to Blaze."

Blaze was on a phone call that seems to have struck yet another nerve. He was ranting and raving about the same problem. Money. Ritza loved the business man in him. She knew that she would be fine as long as the flow of his ends remained endless. "Bay, I am going to the car. Hurry it up."

Blaze glared at her backside. "This bitch must be crazy! Hurry up. I'mma let you have that one cause what I am about to get from you is priceless.....humph...hurry up."

Ritza didn't know how she was going to tell Blaze that she had a temporary solution. She hated to see her man stress.

RIDE TO DIE CHIC 2

There has got to be a way to help Blaze. She thought about what Cinnamon said about them wanting young girls. She decided to recruit a squad of her own. She'd be sort of a pimpette. She popped her collar and chuckled. "I can do this. Sumthin like a pimp, huh." She rushed in the house to tell Blaze his problems were over. She knew so many young girls who would love to make some dough. All she had to do is sell them Prada dreams and Gucci pocketbooks wishes.

Blaze continued talking on the phone walking aimlessly in the foyer shaking his head and occasionally throwing his hands in the air. She never noticed he'd gotten louder once she entered the room. "Blaze, I think..." He held his finger up to her and mouthed wait a minute. She sat on the steps anxiously waiting. He continued to pace back and force screaming and yelling.

"I need my money man! Don't make me break my foot off in your ass man. I don't need this shit! You gonna make me catch a muh fuckin case! What? What?" Blaze threw the phone against the wall and roared. It sent chills throughout Ritza's body. At that point she knew it wasn't the time to tell him about her plan. "Ritz, go upstairs, our date is canceled." She slowly stood smoothing out her dress, just as she was about to turn to him to say goodnight he spazzed. "Just go Ritz, I don't

41

need that puppy dog eye shit. I got money problems..." Ritza nodded and headed to her room. She wished she could sooth his pain like her mother did when Red was upset but she remembered Blaze telling her she had to be of age. "I guess age is more than a number."

TRIFE LIFE TO THE LAVISH

Fallon filled out Ritza's clothes perfectly, but her sneakers were run down. She could hear her classmates laughing at her. "Look at Fallon, she's such a bum. Her sister is always fly and she looks like a rag doll." Frustrated with her appearance Fallon stripped down to her worn bra and panties and sat back on the closet floor. She couldn't believe how Ritza never kept good on her promises. She wept until day break.

RIDE TO DIE CHIC III

Ritza sat on her bed and watched the sun rise. She needed to go to her old stomping ground to find her some young pussy willing to give it up for the lifestyle she would promise them. She'd soon be 16 and she knew a few girls her age and a year older that would die to be in her Jimmy Choos. There wasn't much you wouldn't do as a teen with crackhead parents. They set the precedence of how you did things.

Ritza stood up and headed to her closet. As she looked at all that Blaze bought for her, she wondered how Fallon was doing. She thought about her lil' sis all the time but always pushed her situation to the back of her mind. She'd been building a complete wardrobe for Fallon and now was the time to bring her the stuff since Blaze's money was low and she didn't know when her allowance was going to stop. So she decided to wait. Again.

Ritza didn't want to bother Odessa or Blaze. It was early and she wanted to surprise Blaze with the new idea she had partially in play. Odessa always wanted to tag along during the day so Ritza made it her business to get dressed a little earlier than usual. She peeked out of the window hoping that the car Blaze allowed her to drive was not blocked in. Just as she was about to come out of the window she spotted a grungy white man jumping the side fence. He was too mangy

44

to be a cop; resembling more of a fiend. Ritza then saw him pull out a long metal stick and headed towards the cars. Ritza thought back to Blaze stressing his debt and immediately thought the man was there to take back Blaze's car. Ritza slipped out her room and made her way downstairs.

What the hell? Why aren't the alarms going off?

The click on the front door opening sounded like a mini explosion more so than a slight click. It seems like when you're sneaking every sound you make echoes into the atmosphere. Just as the man's body emerged from the other side of the car Ritza cleared her throat startling the sneak. "Um, can I help you? Seems like your fucking with my property." Ritza kept one hand in her pocket as if she concealed a weapon. This had no bearing on the grungy man now standing just 6ft away from her.

"Fuck you think I'm doing?" He signaled for his friend to pull up from down the block. Shortly a tow truck appeared. "Pay your way and I wouldn't be here. Unless..." Ritza relaxed her attack mode and took her hand out of her pocket. It was clear to her that he didn't fear her one bit. If anything he seemed aroused as he looked her from head to toe; tight jeans and three button shirt that held up her boobs like she was serving them to the onlooker.

"Unless?" She asked not really understanding what he was insinuating by holding his crotch as if he was weighing his balls.

"Unless you want give up some of that tender touch." He eyed her, now cupping underneath his sack and lifting it to make it appear larger than the package.

"Tender touch? Oh no boo-boo...never this." Ritza back up shaking her finger.

"Oh well say bye-bye to your properties. I can tell these here rides have a man's touch. He aint gonna be a happy camper. Lucky we caught the kid."

Grungy now leaned back talking to his approaching partner. Dang! I should have just got one of the girls up. I know if I go back in Blaze is gonna wake and no telling what type of shit he'll get in with these two nutzos. "How about..." Ritza dug into her pockets.

"Baby girl, money ain't in the negotiations. Tender touch or become lil Kim and rock the Mic!" Ritza gasped; her mouth remained open. "Yeah baby love, I'll take that in exchange but you gotta hit my man off too." Ritza's mind raced. She debated on giving up some head or giving up the tail. "We ain't got all day. Dis here is bizness." For

45

some reason his voice seemed to escalate. She knew if he got any louder he would wake Blaze or one of the girls. Either way Blaze would be awakened. Ritza stepped off of the porch and signaled for them to follow her around back. They followed her watching her plump round ass bounce firmly. "Damn Lil Mama, I think I shouldah went with the cooch." He tried to reach out and tap her on the ass.

"Niggah, if the fuck you do. Now shhhh!" Ritza tip-toed to the back yard by the storage house. Naïve and inexperienced Ritza fumbled with the first man's pants. He shooed her hands, unzipped his pants and for the first time she saw a man's private. She winced at how wormy and small it was. There was more hair than dick. This is all. I can do this. Ritza coached herself, closed her eyes and got on her knees.

"Grab it. How you gonna..." Before he could get his words out Ritza was already on the job. He immediately became erect. She was surprised that it grew and inch or two and how hard it was. It made it less disgusting. She sucked and sucked like it was a lollypop only licking the top. "Nah girl, slurp it. Suck it back and forth like a Bomb Pop."

Ritza took him out of her mouth and mumbled. "Bomb Pop...yeah right." But she did as told. He tutored her for about two more minutes and then grabbed the back of her head until he shot in her mouth. She spat. "Oh hell no!"

"That's what your smart ass mouth gets ya. Now you're a graduate with a 3.5." The other guys already had his dick in his hand nearly knocking Ritza over when she saw how large and long he was.

"What the fuck? How am I gonna..." without hesitation the second man stuffed the first five inches of his dick in her mouth. She gagged almost choking on its girth.

"Slow your roll, baby girl. This here will put you head of your class, if you can take this all in. The trick is to relax your throat muscles like you do when you're taking a big ass horse pill." Ritza took his advice. He wasn't as bad looking as the first guy and he smelled cleaner too. Ritza now took him in inch by inch. No longer was she a throat virgin she held on to his shaft and slowly developed a rhythm. She slurped without coaxing. She even enjoyed it watching him squirm as his knees occasionally buckled.

"Damn baby! Your mouth is hot like cayenne pepper." Ritza licked the head and tasted a little of the salty dew seeping from the head. She was intrigued by his taste. She tickled the head of his dick more and sucked the tip. He yelped. She hit him with her free hand as a threat that she would stop if he made any more noise. "Ok baby...sorry." He whispered still shivering from the head she was controlling. She licked the sides of his dick wondering just how long his dick measured out. She curled her tongue grasping his length and bobbed her head in and out until he couldn't take much more. She learned from the former that he was about to release in her mouth but this time she welcomed his hands at the back of her head and she suck every drop from him when she was just about done he fell to his knees surrendering. "Damn! That was the best fucking head I ever got!"

The first man felt jilted. He walked towards her angrily. "You gonna suck my shit like that!" Ritza jumped to her feet in fear. But out of respect for the young girl's gangtsa head the younger dude stopped him.

"Let's go Heff. She did what you asked. You know you ain't working with much!" he smirked. As they emerged from the back of the house the front door opened startling Ritza. Odessa was about to speak but Ritza gave her no chance to ask anything.

"So everything is okay right Mr. Heff. We straight?" It seemed like Heff was gonna leak their secret so she continued. "...or do I owe you one?" She said licking her lips as she faced them with her back towards Odessa. Heff thought about the head she gave his boy and nodded.

"You can pay me my fee when I see you again." She nodded.

"Thanks for the hook up." Heff and his partner left the yard. Ritza walked back in the house passing Odessa. Odessa pulled her back.

"They were gonna take the rides, huh?" Ritza nodded. "Next time let the girls handle that." Ritza looked forward in shame. She knew Dessa knew something.

"I didn't...all I." Dessa rubbed her arm.

"I don't need to know."

DOWN IN THE DIRTY

Ritza drove into the belly of the beast, a hot crack spot where the rows of houses all seemed to be the same color; dirty. She spotted her prey and moved in on her. Letti had a beautiful face. Her baby face is what kept her boosting game a float. Store clerks never paid her any attention assuming she was with a parent. Letti would be a challenge since Ritza couldn't fill her head with material things. What Letti wanted was a sure fire way out of her mother's house and a place that was safe for her baby.

Ritza slowed up as she got closer. "What's up Chicas? I see you are still living in the belly of the beast, huh?" Letti didn't bother to look at the person driving the car she was stuck on the shinning rims. "Girl, it's me; Ritza." Letti looked up from the rims. They never really got down like that because Letti was always looking for her next clothing order, but they knew each other well enough.

"Ritz? Is that you? Where you been?" Ritza put the car in park and hopped out. There was no mistaking that she had made it out of the belly. Her style was high-end. Not hood high end but got a paper chasing man high end. "Yo, you're rocking those Tahari's and you know I know my shoes. Dang bitch who put you on?" Ritza kneeled down to see Letti's daughter. "Girl she's with my friend. This is an order. You know how I do?" Ritza laughed.

48

"So where you living Letti? Matter of fact how are you living? I remember you saying when your daughter was about to be born you were moving out "the belly". This ain't nowhere to live with your lil' girl. We both know that." Ashamed that she still hadn't found a way out Letti didn't even bother to front.

"Yea, every time I get my dough up my mom either is about to get evicted or she finds it and smokes it up. This boosting thang ant what it seems. Bitches are yanking their own shit nowadays. Most of my old customers are either in jail or doing their own thang. It keeps me and my daughter fly a few boutiques and that's about it."

"Take this ride with me. I need to find Ming. She still live down the way?" Ritza emptied the stroller in the trunk, folded it up and slammed it shut. "Ride shot gun with me."

"First we gotta pick up my baby." She ran down what most of the girls were doing in the belly. Even though Letti stayed fly growing up she still recognized who had parents neglecting their daughters. She even named Ming and her friends "Fix'em Up Girls". She always said if she fixed them up they would be beauties.

"So Ming, still hanging with the "Fix Em Up Girls"? I think I got a way to get us all paid and you guys out of the belly." Letti was all ears.

"Girl where did you come up with this idea?"

"Girl If I tell you I'mma haftah kill ya." Letti sat back and pondered on the thought.

"Turn here."

"Where, Letti?" Letti pointed to the last driveway on Fifth Street right before the curve in the road.

"Pull in." Letti was adamant that this was the address.

"Letti, this house aint been lived in since it caught fire when I was damn near five."

Letti gave Ritza a look that said "I know what you mean but yea, this is the place." Ritza beeped the horn, windows half cracked then a curvy young Chinese girl waltzed out to the car in dingy pajama pants and a tank top not large enough to hold her double D's.

"My mom said this is all she has. Can she get an eight ball?"

"Girl if you don't put that away. It's me Ritza and Letti. I've got a proposition for you." Ming stepped back took in the fly ride.

"Yo! Really? Ritz this you? I heard you was with that pimp ass niggah Blaze, but I didn't believe it. How many dicks did you have to suck to get this?" Letti was just about to flip on Ming but Ritza

49

stopped her mouthing; I got this. Ritza put her personal feelings aside and road with Ming on her assumption.

"Not too many! But enough to keep me laced up!" Ming's eyes widened as she leaned in to take in Ritza's jewelry and gear.

"Yo! You looking good as fuck, Put me on." Although Ming was half joking Ritza was all the way serious.

"Boo-Boo, that's was a good fuck gets you! Whatchoo do best? "A" Games or Head game?"

Ritza looked over at Letti who nodded and raised her pinky. Ritza met her pinkie and interlocked it with Letti's. From there a new bond of respect was formed. Letti looked back at her daughter and smiled warmly. She thought to herself, never another hungry night! "Where we headed?"

"To the top, bitches!"

Ritza was mapping her game plan as she went along. It was as if the bricks were being laid before her and all she had to do was keep moving forward. "So what are you to that niggah Blazin'? His bottom bitch?"

Ritza laughed. "It's Blaze!"

"Nah I seen that niggah before. It's Blazin'!" Ritza made a mental note to keep Ming as far away from Blaze as possible.

"Boundaries, bitch. Boundaries, and that's rule number one!" Ming pouted and sat back. Letti saw the vision Ritza had coming to pass. She could see dollar signs form in Ming's eyes.

"Mami, next stop Suggettes Lane." Ritza nodded at Letti's directions.

"Just tell me where and when to turn."

Not before long Ritza had a car full of soon to be Top Bitches! Everyone served their purpose. Ming would be the number one top bitch. She would need to be trained on etiquette and poise but her ethnicity and curvy body would be the hook. Letti would always dress her Geisha style.

Johnah had the youngest face even though she was the oldest. She rarely talked. She was deaf, living with deaf parents there was little need to. She was shy but had lip reading skills and instinct. She would be trained to do the dirtiest deed.

Tuka always bullied everyone. She grew up defensive because she was a product of physical abuse. Her fist game was ferocious although she barely stood 5 feet. Her backside was voluptuous, waist little but had that smart girl appeal. She read constantly; escaping the crack world that she was constantly forced to live in. When they picked her up she was sitting on the stoop reading Who Do You Love? by Shadress Denise.

Mush was the verbal mouth piece. She could talk a teacher out of his T.E.A.C and make it all about HER. The gift of gab would get us into places we had no business being; age restricted.

After running down the rules of the game and what she had to offer she dropped everyone off where she picked them up with a head full of fluff and dreams of cash money except Letti.

"Letti I never had any friends growing up and I think you and me can hit it off." Ritza looked over her shoulder through the rear view mirror taking in the smiles and gurgles of Letti's daughter. "The game starts and stops with us! You do this so she doesn't have to. I do this so Fallon will never have to. I don't want you tricking. Keep your snatch for scratch game and dress the girls. I like your style and you keep it a hundred. You could have ran your mouth back then but you let me know that you saw what I saw, so that made us official. Plus you got lil Lettie. I just ask that you not take her anymore when you shop. Take two of the best boosters with you and I will put them on once they show their dedication. Let's say a "G" a week. Some days they will be just plotting. No more going in not knowing."

Letti was teary eyed. "Thanks Ritza, I didn't know how I was going to pull it off. I have had sex three times and got pregnant and said no more. So, I got this. Tell me what you mean by plotting." Ritza explained how they would ride from upstate Connecticut back to Bridgeport hitting their target mark. So if Donna Karen had stores from upstate to Bridgeport they were going to hit them in the worse way. The first few times they would spend in one store and return in the next and keep the pattern just to case out the way they operated and the workers patterns and then reverse it back upstate. The only thing that would switch would be the shifts. So they didn't wear out their newness.

"Damn Ritza you mapped this shit out to the "T"." Letti felt safe for the first time in years. If only she could get out of her moms' house. Where would she keep her inventory? "Tomorrow be ready early. Put on some grown mama shit and bring Letisha. We have an apartment to rent." Letti turned to Ritza and grinned.

"Oh! It's on!"

Discussion Questions

1. Do you believe we model behaviors for our children? If so do you not believe that "Do as I say not as I do!" and "I do this so you don't have to!" works or is understood by our children?

2. Ritza seems to be very carefree about the world she sees Blaze live in. Do you think that is why she was so easily and ready and willing to join the game herself? Or do you think she was only thinking of a way to survive?

3. Our children run make friends in school with children from all backgrounds. Do you think exposure to the fast life looking from outside seems glamorous to our daughters more so than our sons?

4. How do you think Ritza is going to pull off her get money scheme? What do you think she is going to start with these talented girls?

5. She speaks about what she is planning for Fallon but why do you think she has yet to send her anything?

Felisha is willing to hold discussions on these questions and questions of your own. Please contact her at: publicirty@urbangrapevinemag.com or simply inbox her at www.facebook.com/felisha.bradshaw. She is currently at her max in friends, but please by all means follow her and send her a message.

PART TWO
Handed Down
When hand me downs are no longer needed!

Coming Soon

....Previously in Hand Me Downs

Update:

Ritza goes back to her neighborhood as a solution to Blaze's so called money problems. She recruits a team of fix 'em up girls from the belly of the beast and teaches them how to use their hand me downs to get money. With Odessa and Ritza's team of girls from the belly, she knew this was a trim wins situation.

Episode Two Continues... (after this commercial)

FLY GIRL FLY BETTY

"**W**here you been ma?" Blaze asked from the top of the staircase. He tried to hide his frustration knowing he wanted to teach her a lesson but refrained.

"Finding a solution to our money problems. I gottah do what I needs to do for you first, baby!" Blaze forgotten that this chic was a rare breed and was nothing like his other bitches. He was beginning to see her in a new light; breaking rule number one in the pimp game.

1. Never see any of your bitches as that bitch!

As he jogged down the steps he asked, "Well you gonna leave a niggah hanging or you gonna tip me on how you plan to do that?" He wasn't sleeping her abilities any longer. She did pass the first test; saving his vehicles.

"Baby, let me get this shit like I need to, so I can show you I ain't just some ordinary chic. All I am asking is that you trust me boo, like I trust you. All I need is three g's and I will flip it in a week." Blaze aint never before put cash in any bitches hand but for some reason he believed Ritza's and was curious to find out if she could deliver.

"That's a serious dent in my pockets ma! But I got this feeling you gonna bring us back to life. I'mma plug you in." A week from that day was Ritza's 16th birthday.

Blaze lifted Ritza carrying her into the den. "Damn. Baby you got my head fucked up." He dropped her on the couch lightly and flicked on the television. "I'mma rock with you today. I sent the girls with Dessa to work a massage parlor to make up for their shorts. So, you got me till about eight-ish." Ritza loved the down time with Blaze it was what she called their date time. "You wanna order in?" Blaze accompanied Ritza on the sofa, leaned forward, lifted the ottoman in front of him to get take out menus

"Nope! I got a better idea." Ritza planted a kiss on his forehead and walked off. When he started to follow her she stopped. "Go ahead and flick on the game. I'mma be back in about an hour. Enjoy Bae, today I'mma make it about you. When do you ever get a "all about Blaze day?" Blaze grinned. For the first time ever a woman thought about him first, not his pockets, not his drugs, not for her benefit sexually but just because she wanted to do something nice for him. Yes, Ritza was a rare breed.

"Ok Ma, you go ahead and do your thang. I'll be right here watching the ball game till you get back." Blaze made comfy on the oversized sofa. This was his first day off in 5 years. Nothing to do, nowhere to go and no one to look over or after. He didn't know what to do with himself. It didn't take long before he was out like a light in total comfort while the game watched him.

Odessa stood in the foyer absorbing every word. She smiled at the fact that Blaze indeed had his hands full. She hopped up the steps three at a time. The girls were working and it was Odessa's personal time. Normally she would spend this with her son; Aria`n, but he was in therapy. She wanted to go into Blaze's emergency stash to peel off a few thousand to send to Aria`n's group home for additional therapeutic classes outside of what Blaze pays. Every other month she'd dip into his money to send to the group home. She'd used her side hustles to buy him the extra things he wanted. Aria`n was a music prodigy so she kept him with state of the art technology. Since Blaze was asleep she figured now would be a better time than any.

After going into his hiding spot she went to handle some business she had on the side. Heading back to her room she went into her walk in closet and moved her winter clothes rack to get to the back wall she removed the sheet rock and pulled out her Visio laptop it enter and the screen came up. There was a clear view of all bedrooms. Blaze's, Ritza's, and his three tricks excluding her own. She hit rewind and watched Blaze mutilate a very young girl's pussy. He must have banged her in every position imaginable and some he created from his twisted mind. The young girl took it like a trooper. She saved it to the archives then went into a shoe box for a memory stick downloaded it again for insurance and then went to Ritza's room to watch the footage; nothing worth taping. Damn he ain't hit that yet? Ritz baby you's a brain!

The trick's footage was normally the same; they fucked each other they fucked Odessa, they fucked Blaze. But then Nyla the youngest of them; just a ripe 22 years old had unexpected company. Odessa couldn't make out the voice but then a male's body was in view but his face continued a mystery throughout the entire footage. The things he had Nyla do were indescribable. Damn Nyla! Does Blaze even know about this, because his number two rule was no business brought in the house? He was a weed addict but he only brought one blunt for the night. How'd she even get this guy in without me knowing? She shook her head. You never shit and piss where you sleep or eat!

Odessa replaced the sheetrock and her clothing rack still baffled by what she uncovered. It stayed heavy on her mind for all of twenty seconds. Nyla was nothing but another young trick with a habit trying to get that extra. She'd been taping everyone for over a year for what she called quality assurance. She left the house undetected.

Ritza was doing her thing in the kitchen She loved cooking. She prepared a feast for two kings. She sautéed roast beef in red wine red onions and red peppers and pepper jack cheese. She seasoned three different potatoes; red, Idaho and sweet and sliced them into homemade fries smothered in Velveeta melted cheese and Hormel Chili. She made dip and filled a bowl with assorted chips, gather two enormous mugs with A&W Root Beer. She tiptoed her way in and out of the room setting up the coffee table just in time for the next game to start.

"Bae!" She planted kisses on his cheek as she plopped down beside him. He grunted and shifted his weight turning his body towards her. She rubbed his face, leaned in and whispered, "Blaaaaze, wake up!"

Blaze slowly opened his eyes looking up at Ritza. "Have I been sleeping long? Did I miss game two?" He sat up and was quickly taken back by the feast before him. "Damn baby! Where did you order this from?"

Ritza frowned. "Ordered? I made this for you!" Blaze straightened up, looked in Ritza's face and saw that she was dead ass serious.

"Really, lil' mama you did this for me? Even the loaded fries?" Ritza smiled proudly. "Wow! Thanks Ma, you staying with me right?" Ritza pulled off her shirt to reveal her favorite team logo on her tank top. Blaze reared back laughing holding his stomach with a mouth full of fries. "Ohhhhhh, so uddah enemy huh?"Ritza looked at him seriously.

"Nah Bookie, just different teams. I will never be the enemy!" She kissed him and grabbed her sandwich. He was stuck for a second looking at the new shorty beside him. "I gotchoo!" She smiled.

"And I gotcho!"

For Release Date
www.IAmAuthorFBradshaw.com

Turn The Page
For A **SNEAK PEEK** of The
Latest Release From

SHADRESS DENISE

BLUE INDIGO PUBLISHING PRESENTS

Who Do You Love Too?

SHADRESS DENISE

Who Do You Love Too?

SHADRESS DENISE

Blue Indigo Publishing

© 2015 Blue Indigo Publishing
© 2015 Shadress Denise

ISBN-13: 978-0692566671
ISBN-10: 0692566678

Editor| Shelby Lazenby |Progressive Editing Solutions, LLC
Book Cover Designer| Dynastys CoverMe | www.dynastyscoverme.com
Interior Design|Strawberry Publications, LLC
www.StrawberryPublications.com

Also written by Shadress Denise

Disturbia
Who Do You Love?

Prologue

his is my drug, my vice, my daily habit, or
whatever you may want to classify it as. It is the only
thing that allows me to function from day-to-day. It is my
poison, which gives me extreme highs not even marijuana can achieve.

I craved pleasure.

At times I desired to be fucked, yet there is a small portion of me
buried deep in my core that often seeks love and intimacy. Slow
whispers make their way to the surface as Anais' words find comfort
on my earlobe; the only abnormality is the inability to love.

I reach for it. It hesitates.

My body is content with this arrangement.

My soul straddles the fence.

My heart doesn't trust me at all.

It battles with lust, and at times it often loses.

Moments when orgasms cloud my judgment, I forget I was even
fighting for love. I struggled with fighting for a balance between sanity
and insanity. At this moment, what this man was doing to me clearly
declared a victory for lust and a loss for love. He ravished me like a
man who craved control. His touches resembled a wild being that
wallowed in the mere presence of dominance. I loved dominant sex,
though there was something different about this. It seemed foreign,
like I had never experienced this side of him before.

It was uncivilized and untamed.

He was a predator who knew he had finally caught his prey.

I had a million things going on with my body at one time. The alcohol and controlled substances I partook of earlier with Asha at the Omega party were taking its toll on me. Initially, it started off with just a couple of shots, somehow it ended up being a few more shots that turned into a couple hits off a blunt. On top of the narcotics in my system, I added half an ecstasy pill.

Asha was a horrible influence on me. Usually I was the bad influence, however tonight she held the title. By the time she placed it in my hand it was already too late. The subdued state I was in now controlled my every move. I left the party only to show up at his place. It seemed the only reasoning I had was left at the door.

I didn't want to fight, nor did I want to argue.

My mind was in a different place from our problems.

I had come here to do everything other than talk. Talking was not on the menu tonight. I was missing him, and I needed something to take my mind off of our fight. Hence, the unnatural high I was currently trapped in. Regardless of what was said, I was wrong. I admitted it so I couldn't understand why we were still here. I realized I had hurt him. Another piece of my past showed up, and this time he showed up with a ring. We had just moved past the whole me lying thing, and we were right back to square one. I should have listened to Jay and told him the truth. I should've told him when the first set of flowers showed up on my doorstep.

Now we were at this point. Me begging for forgiveness with silent pleas of pleasures, while he showed me no mercy as he pulled them out of me.

I placed my hands on the shower door, and slow breaths fled my soul. I watched the steam cover up the handprints as ecstasy and sin were left behind. I gripped the bars as he entered me, greedily. Withdrawals had a way of consuming you. They never laid dormant for long. Eventually, you will have to feed them. You would somehow have to submit to the control they had over you.

He gripped my throat as I slid against the shower wall. The coolness of the glass made me flinch as the hot water ran down my face. I could hear the streaking sound my fingertips made against the glass. I wanted this in the worst way. In a way that was so illegal that it should be outlawed.

He looked at me, and I could see there was something different in his eyes. There was passion lingering upon the surface. Then there was a hunger, a possessiveness lying beneath all of it. At this very moment, we weren't making love, we were flat out fucking.

It was carnal. It was raw.

I was unconcealed, and unwilling to be caged.

It was unforgiving, and left no questions unanswered.

Our sex had never been this aggressive before. Traces of zealous violence gradually seeped through. Nonetheless, my sweet spot responded to each aggressive stroke he gave me. I was inhaling a new high that was destined to leave me with dangerous withdrawals. I was riding a wave that would soon carry me away. A new standard was being set. A new standard that I would be expecting every time we gave into our desires.

Smoke gray eyes were staring at me.

Water ran down his chocolate skin.

Well-defined muscles contracted as he forcibly held me up.

My airway was fighting for relief. My chest was pleading for me to slow down my breathing. My eyes were blurry as the water fell on my face. I wanted to wipe it away, but I decided it wasn't important. I used the strength I had left in my arms to hold onto him. He pulled out of me, and continued the assault on my sweet spot with his tongue. I stood under the water gasping for air as he lifted my legs and licked me until I yelled out in sweet surrender. My eyes rolled to the back of my head. I exhaled the deep moan I had been holding in. If that was the last breath I would ever release I would be fine with it.

I looked down as his head moved in and out. He was torturing what was left of my resolve. I blinked a couple of times to make sure I wasn't seeing things. I was tipsy and high as hell, though that mark had never been there before. It had been a couple of weeks since we had crossed paths. I figured maybe it was something new, and I could worry about it later.

I closed my eyes, drifting into euphoria as the orgasmic cloud I was on carried me away. There was something about this, about him that seemed twisted. Somehow I didn't care. I gripped what I knew to be my lover's head as he pulled out the demon buried within me. He took complete control of me.

Whatever happened after this no longer mattered.

My secrets were no longer a factor.

He held my need for pleasure in the palms of his hands.
I could die right now and be a happy woman.

We hope you have enjoyed the Sneak Peek into Who Do You Love Too?
More about the author www.iamshadressdenise.com

www.ingramcontent.com/pod-product-compliance
Lightning Source LLC
Chambersburg PA
CBHW061453170626
46811CB00004B/1487